Hugh Hiccups

'I'm afraid I've got hiccups,' said Hugh.
'I just don't know what I can do.
I keep going "hic", I feel dreadfully sick.
I wish I could stop,' hiccupped Hugh.

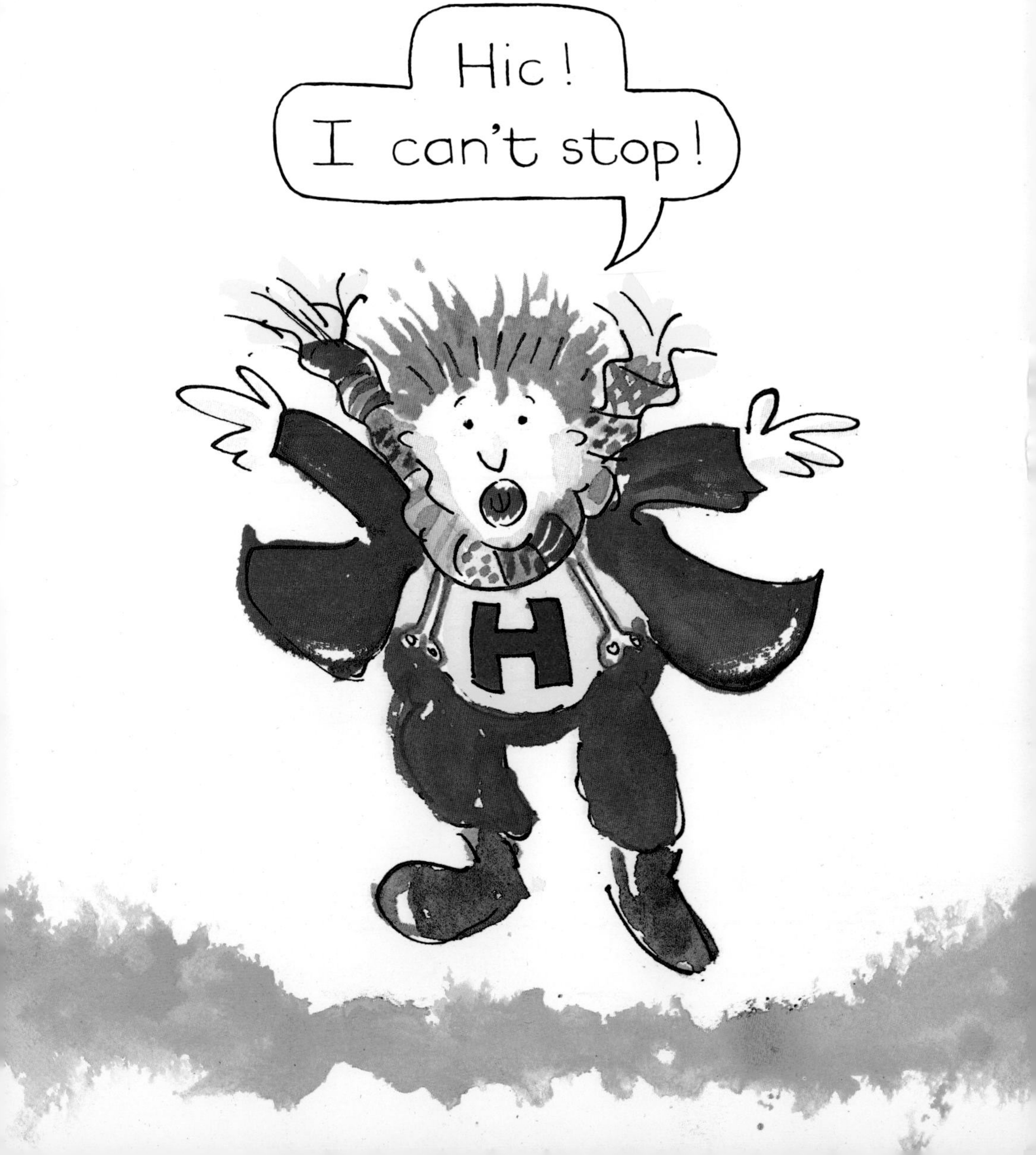
Hic! I can't stop!

'Oh dear Auntie Hattie,' he cried,
'Is there anything I haven't tried?'
'Well I once knew a cure, but I can't be quite sure.
We'll look in my book – it's inside.'

'Ah yes, "Cures for Hiccups" – let's see.
They're numbered here one, two and three.
First stand on your head, and eat honey on bread.
And look out in case there's a bee!'

Poor Hugh tried it out for a day.
But his hiccups did not go away.
'My head is so sore, this honey's a bore.
I'd like to give up, if I may!'

'We'll have to try Cure Number Two.
I don't know what else we can do.
It says, "Hop up a hill, then stand very still".'
'That sounds very easy,' said Hugh.

'But wait! You must put on your head
Five herrings all smelly and dead.
If you keep them on and ignore their strong pong,
The hiccups will vanish, it's said!'

Put five herrings
on your head.

So Hugh bravely hopped up the hill,
But the herrings they wouldn't keep still.
'Take the pin from my hat, and pin them with that.'
'Their smell makes me feel rather ill.'

'Don't worry, just leave it to me.
We'll try the next cure, let me see . . .
"Count the hairs on a horse, but remember of course
Don't stop till five hundred and three".'

Hugh hoped this would soon do the trick.
'I just can't keep on going "hic".
Oh dear Auntie Hattie, I think I'll go batty!'
Just then the huge horse gave a kick.

Poor Hugh shot up high in the air.
Auntie Hattie looked on in despair.
That horse with its hoof sent Hugh over the roof.
'Oh Hugh!' shouted Auntie, 'Take care!'

She watched how he span round and round.
Would he land on the house or the ground?
He just missed the veg, and came down in a hedge,
And let out a hair-raising sound.

'I've sat on some holly!' cried Hugh.
'I'm sure I am pricked through and through!'
'But you've stopped going "hic", that kick did the trick!'
'By golly, by goodness, that's true!'

You've stopped going 'hic'!

Cure
A shock.